anythink

D0118911

To Donna

SMcB

For Vikki

AJ

First US edition 2020

Library of Congress Catalog Card Number pending
ISBN 978-1-5362-1747-6

20 21 22 23 24 25 CCP 10 9 8 7 6 5 4 3 2 1

Printed in Shenzhen, Guangdong, China

This book was typeset in Cochin.
The illustrations were done in ink and watercolor.

Candlewick Press
99 Dover Street
Somerville, Massachusetts 02144

www.candlewick.com

WILL YOU BE MY FRIEND?

illustrated by

Sam McBratney Anita Jeram

Candlewick Press

Little Nutbrown Hare
wanted to play, but there was much
to be done and Big Nutbrown Hare
was very busy.

"Can I go and play by myself?"
asked Little Nutbrown Hare.
"Well, yes," said Big Nutbrown Hare,
"but don't go too far."

"I won't!" said Little Nutbrown Hare.

And off he hopped to explore on his own.

Soon he discovered a puddle.

There was another hare in the puddle, staring up at him. That's all it did: it just stared.

"You're only another me!"
said Little Nutbrown Hare.

He poked the puddle with his ears
and skipped on down
the path.

Then Little Nutbrown Hare spotted his shadow.
There it was, on the ground, quite still.

"I'll race you!"
said Little Nutbrown Hare.

Up and away he went, but of course,
his shadow went too—and just as quickly.

You're only another me!
thought Little Nutbrown Hare.

Still exploring, Little Nutbrown Hare
soon came to Cloudy Mountain.

What a surprise he found
there in the heather!

Someone was looking straight at him.

Someone *real*!

"Hello," said Little Nutbrown Hare.

"My name is Tipps," said
the Cloudy Mountain Hare.
"Will you be my friend?
Do you want to play?"

Yes, thought Little Nutbrown Hare.

I *do* want to play.

They chased each other
through the heather.

They dug a deep hole

and built a pile high.

They had
tremendous
fun together.

Then they raced up Cloudy Mountain
for a game of hide-and-seek.
Tipps lay down low in the heather
and waited.

Little Nutbrown Hare hid among the rocks,

and *he* waited.

He was sure that his friend would come looking for him.

He waited for ages, until
it was time to go home.
But Tipps didn't come.

Where, he wondered,
was his friend Tipps?
Would he see her again?
He didn't know.

Big Nutbrown Hare was pleased
to see Little Nutbrown Hare come home.

"And how did your exploring go?"
he asked.

"Good. It was good exploring,"
said Little Nutbrown Hare.

And then, close by, they heard a noise.

Was someone coming?

“It’s a little snow hare!” said Big Nutbrown Hare.
“Now, where on earth did she come from?”

Little Nutbrown Hare smiled.

He knew.

"She's from
Cloudy Mountain.
Her name is
Tipps—and she's
my friend."